The
Ultimate
Hair Guide

by Karen Tina Harrison

 A GOLDEN BOOK · NEW YORK
Golden Books Publishing Company, Inc.,
New York, New York 10106

Art Direction by Ellen Jacobs
Design by Tanya Mauler

Photography of hairstyles on pages 16–28 by James Levin

Hairstyles on pages 16–28 by Clare Lichtenberger
and Lana G. for Lana G. and Company

Illustrations by Joann Owen Coy

GOLDEN BOOKS®, A GOLDEN BOOK®, G DESIGN®, and the
distinctive gold spine are trademarks of Golden Books Publishing
Company, Inc. Library of Congress Catalog Card Number: 97-80599
ISBN: 0-307-30400-0   A MCMXCVIII

Hi!

Welcome to THE ULTIMATE HAIR GUIDE!
This is a book that will help you
make your hair look totally cool.
It's packed with styling ideas,
hair crafts, and hair care tips
galore! And it's all easy,
fast, and fun.

You know, no matter what
kind of hair you have, you
can be stylin'! Plus, it's fun
to take care of your hair!
So let's have some fun!

Love,
Barbie

Hair Care

Hair Health

The first step toward beautiful hair is healthy hair. You get healthy hair by eating balanced meals, exercising, getting lots of sleep, and drinking enough water. What's good for your body is also good for your hair!

I always eat lots of fruits and vegetables!

Grow, Girl!

Scientists haven't found any miracle foods that make your hair grow faster or thicker. But when you get enough vitamins you grow strong hair. And strong hair grows about half an inch a month!

Water That Puppy!

Drink plenty of water. Water keeps your skin from drying out, so it will keep your scalp moisturized, too!

I try to drink eight glasses of water every day.

Hints

Pump It!

Exercise makes your heart beat faster and your blood circulate better. Good circulation delivers nutrients to your scalp and helps new hair grow.

Rub-a-Dub

Some people claim that scalp massages make your hair grow faster. There is no proof that they actually work, but they feel great! Gently rub your fingertips in small circles all over your scalp. You and your best bud can trade giving each other massages.

Cool Hair Factoid:

Did you know that your body, including your hair, grows the most when you're asleep?

Work it, girls!

Clean and Shiny Hair

For healthy hair to look totally rad, it needs to be clean. Clean hair is shiny, full, and easier to style.

Shampoo Smarts

Your scalp produces natural oils that help it stay soft and shiny. Some girls can go only one day before their hair gets oily. For other girls it can take two or three days. But any more than that and yuck—oil city! Time for a wash!

People used to think it was good to shampoo every day. But too much shampooing can leave your hair dry and your scalp itchy. So what do you do? Shampoo as needed. It's that simple. Every girl is unique. And every girl knows what feels right for her.

A rule of thumb: Always shampoo after swimming. Salt and chlorine are bad for everyone's hair!

I use a shower cap to keep my hair dry in the bath or shower when I don't need a shampoo.

Kinds of Shampoo

There are many different kinds of shampoos. Most of these shampoo types are for grown-ups, although they won't hurt your hair if you use them. If you have a choice, stick with the kind for normal hair. Or try a kids' shampoo—it's gentler on the hair and won't sting if you get it in your eyes. Follow the shampooing directions on the bottle.

Kelly and Stacie always use kids' shampoo because it smells great! And I like it, too!

Cool Hair Factoid:

Yo! Did you know that shampoo and conditioner build-up can make your hair look gross and keep new hair from growing? Avoid build-up by making sure you don't use too much of either product, and rinse well.

Condition It!

You can also use conditioner in your hair after you shampoo. Conditioner makes your hair extra shiny and loosens the knots. Most kids' shampoos have conditioner built in, which makes shampooing and conditioning a one-step process. But you can also get a separate conditioner. Follow the directions on the bottle.

Being Different Is Rad!

Hair comes in many cool textures. Which kind do you have?

Fine:	Your strands are very small around.
Coarse:	Your strands are thick and have rough surfaces.
Curly:	Your strands are wavy.
Straight:	Your strands are flat.
Thick:	You have more strands of hair than average.
Thin:	You have fewer strands of hair than average.

Getting It Dry!

You're All Wet!

Healthy hair is pretty strong—that's how it mostly stays in your head and doesn't fall out in huge clumps. Duh! But when it's wet, hair is not as strong. That's when it can be stretched and snapped by rough treatment. So be extra gentle, and use a comb instead of a brush on wet hair.

My hair takes forever to dry!

Dry It, Baby!

Using a blow-dryer is the fastest way to dry your hair. To avoid over-drying, make sure your hair is still slightly damp when you're done. If you blow-dry your own hair, always ask an adult to plug in the dryer. Never, ever blow-dry near a full sink or tub because electricity and water are a dangerous combination!

Letting your hair air-dry is easier. It's also a great way to show off natural curls and waves, or even naturally straight hair. When you air-dry your hair, all you have to do is comb out the tangles and wait. Sometimes, using a towel turban can speed up the process. Just bend down, fold the towel around your hair, twist the towel, and raise your head. It takes practice, but fifteen minutes later, your hair should be almost dry!

Stacie thinks towel turbans look kinda glam.

Fun in the Sun

In warm weather, be sure to protect your hair from getting dried out or bleached by the sun. Some companies make sunscreens especially for hair!

ool Hair Factoid:

Did you know that the weather affects the way your hair looks? Humid air has more water in it. This makes hair bouncier and curlier and causes it to dry more slowly. Dry air makes hair dry faster, but it makes it a little flatter.

I like to wear a hat or use hair gel that contains sunscreen.

Combs and Brushes

Since combs and brushes do different things, it's a good idea to have two different combs and a brush.

Big Teeth—the Better to Comb You With!

One comb should have widely spaced "teeth" for combing out tangles. Skipper uses her wide comb in the shower while she has conditioner in her hair. The conditioner allows the comb to slide right through her hair.

To get rid of snarls, start near the ends of your hair and gently work the comb through the knots. Then move up an inch, and keep doing that until your comb sails through your hair from the roots to the ends.

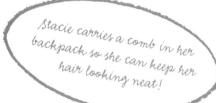

Little Teeth

Fine-tooth combs straighten out the part in your hair. You can also create a new part if you get tired of the old one! Just drag the end of the comb in a line where you want a part and separate the hair along the sides.

Stacie carries a comb in her backpack so she can keep her hair looking neat!

The Best Part

It's easy to tell where your natural part is. When your hair is dry, bend your head and flip your hair down and then back. Your hair will separate at its natural part.

A Brush a Day

You should use a brush for a few moments every day to keep your hair looking healthy and shiny. You can use a brush to make your hair flat and smooth by gently brushing down straight against your scalp. Or you can make your hair puffy and full by bending down and brushing all your hair toward the floor. Then flip up your head and smooth your hair back with your fingers.

Brushes

Brushes come in three basic shapes: paddle, round, and vented.

Paddle brushes are oval-shaped and are good for general smoothing and fluffing.

Round brushes are good for curling. Small round brushes create tight curls, while big ones create loose waves.

Vented brushes are usually rectangular, with bristles on only one side. They work well with a blow-dryer.

Haircut How-to's

Time for a haircut? Short hair should be cut every two months to keep its shape. If you're a long-haired girl like me, you'll need to have the ends trimmed every three months. And if you have bangs, have them trimmed once they hit your eyelids, so you can see! Duh!

My friend Midge chopped off her bangs when we were little, and it took months for her hair to grow back! She was sorry she tried to cut it herself.

Where to Get a Haircut

It doesn't matter which experienced haircutter cuts your hair as long as you are happy with the way it looks!

You can have your hair cut by:
1. an experienced adult in your family
2. a barber at a barbershop
3. a hairstylist at a salon
4. a student hairdresser at a beauty school

Here are some very basic haircuts you can get:

Bang-a-Lang

If your hair is straight, thick bangs look great with any cut. You can also ask a hairstylist or an experienced adult to cut "wispies" for you. These are very thin bangs that you can wear down or swept off your face.

I dig my new bangs!

The Bob

This is a classic haircut in which all of your hair is cut straight across at shoulder length.

The Pixie

For this short style, the hair is cut in very short, shaggy layers around your face, with bangs.

I wore a pixie cut when I was little.

Stylin' Hair

There are many different products that make hair easier to style. Just remember that these products can sometimes stain clothes or other fabrics, so use them carefully. Also make sure to keep them away from your eyes, mouth, and nose.

Gel Is Swell

Hair gel makes your hair stick together and keeps it in place. The perfect time to use gel is when you wear your hair back, because it keeps strands from slipping into your face. For a wet look, use the gel on wet or dry hair and don't blow-dry or comb. For a natural look, use the gel—then blow-dry to hold the style. If you're using curlers, rub a drop of gel along each section before rolling. This will make the curl take hold and last.

Mousse It!

Mousse is a foamy product used to set hair. Use a blob the size of a golf ball and work it through your hair. Then blow-dry or set in curlers.

Just Say Hair Spray

Hair spray helps to keep a hairdo in place when you finish styling it. Spray it lightly over your whole hairdo, avoiding your face. Keep your eyes shut while you spray.

Shine Is Fine

If your clean hair looks dull, you can buy special products that make it shiny. Shiners are often called "pomade." A little bit of shine goes a long way, so don't use too much or your hair might look oily.

Exciting Extras

Most of the styles in this book call for accessories—some basic, some fancy—so here is a round-up. You should try to have a variety of accessories on hand to hold your hair in place when you create new styles.

Skipper, Stacie, Kelly, and I all share accessories so we don't have to buy a lot.

Hair

Beautiful Barrettes

These clip-on accessories come in many beautiful materials and designs. When you shop for barrettes, make sure they have no sharp edges. And if you can, buy a variety of sizes for clipping small or large sections of hair.

Helpful Headbands

Headbands push your hair back off your forehead and come in circles (like sweatbands) or plastic U-shapes.

I wear a headband whe[n] I play tenn[is]

Marvelous Minicombs

These hair helpers are smaller, curved versions of the combs you use to comb your hair. They grip thick or curly hair best.

Accessories

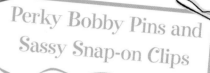

Graceful Ribbons

Ribbons are great because they come in so many fabrics and designs. They can make a hairstyle look fancy or cute, and they can match your outfit to create a cool look.

Kelly loves it when I put ribbons in her hair. They make her feel like a princess.

Perky Bobby Pins and Sassy Snap-on Clips

Bobby pins and clips are good for small jobs, like holding back bangs that are growing out or holding up strands that fall out of upswept 'do's. They come in lots of colors and designs. Try the glittery ones for dressing up!

Skipper and her teenage friends like to wear a bunch of snap-ons together.

Super Scrunchies

When an elastic band is covered by a big, gathered piece of fabric, it's called a "scrunchie." Scrunchies can turn a simple ponytail into a dressed-up hairdo.

Stacie loves to wear scrunchies that match her outfits.

Basic Butterfly Clips

This easy hair holder has two halves that open and close like a butterfly's wings. A butterfly clip is very good for holding big twists of hair.

I use butterfly clips to pull my hair back when I'm busy.

Hairstyle

The Basic Clip

This is the most basic way to style your hair, whether it's long or short: Just part your hair and clip it back with a barrette or two!

Here are some variations on the basic clip:

💜 Clip your hair back very close to your face for a cute look.

💜 Try adding rows of extra barrettes.

💜 Try a middle part if you usually wear it on the side.

Skipper loves changing her part around.

Short Styles

Here are a few basic things you can do with short hair.

Yikes! Spikes!

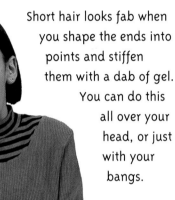

Short hair looks fab when you shape the ends into points and stiffen them with a dab of gel. You can do this all over your head, or just with your bangs.

Proud Cloud

Short, curly hair looks great when you brush it to the top of your head, hold it down flat with a headband or barrettes, and brush the rest of the hair outward.

Babydoll

You don't have to have long hair to wear barrettes. Short hair looks adorable with tiny barrettes clipped in the sides.

Slick Trick

Use gel to comb your hair flat against your head for a sleek, wet look.

Pony Up!
Where's the Pony? On Your Head!

Classy Pony

Make a low ponytail (right where your head and neck meet) and cover the elastic with a big velvet or satin bow.

Half & Half

Make a part across the top of your head from ear to ear. Gather that hair in a ponytail and secure it with a barrette or ribbon-covered elastic. Let the rest of your hair flow free.

Double-Decker

How about wearing your pigtails one atop the other? Make a Half & Half, and then make a ponytail out of the bottom section of hair, too!

The Poodle Pony

Long-haired girls make this ponytail by gathering all their hair in an elastic every three inches and then fluffing out each section with their fingers.

Tales of Pigtales

The classic way to wear pigtails is high above each ear with your hair center-parted from your forehead to your neck.

Kelly's favorite!

Harvest of Hair

This hairdo will bring lots of attention to short or very curly hair. Make at least five "mini-ponies" out of small sections of hair all over your head!

Braid Parade

Braids are popular all over the world. You might need help at first, so ask someone to show you how to braid. Try to practice braiding your friends' hair, too.

I practice on my sisters—Skipper, Stacie, and Kelly.

The Classic Braid

1. Separate a ponytail into three even sections. Keep the sections separate while you braid.

2. Hold the three sections in your hands as shown in the diagram.

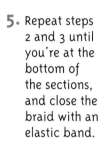

3. Cross the right sections over the center and between the other two sections.

4. Cross the left sections over the center and between the two sections.

5. Repeat steps 2 and 3 until you're at the bottom of the sections, and close the braid with an elastic band.

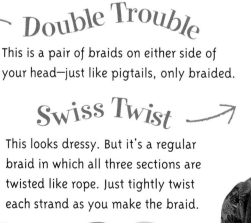

Double Trouble

This is a pair of braids on either side of your head—just like pigtails, only braided.

Swiss Twist

This looks dressy. But it's a regular braid in which all three sections are twisted like rope. Just tightly twist each strand as you make the braid.

Braid Crown

This is a sweet but simple 'do. Gather a section of hair from in front of your ear. Don't put an elastic band at the top. Braid three or four inches of hair, then put an elastic band at the bottom. Repeat on the opposite side. Now gather the two braids at the top of your head, and join them with a beautiful barrette that covers the elastics.

Braid in the Shade

For this style, make a skinny braid from the hair high above one ear—or you can even try both ears!

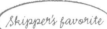

Skipper's favorite

Cornrow Crazy

My favorite

This is a fab hairdo in which short or medium-length hair is tightly braided in lots of tiny rows across your head. Because it's a big project and the braids are small, you need to have someone do it for you. The best part is that you can leave the braids in for weeks and they'll still look good! Just remember to shampoo very gently so the braids don't come undone.

Ooh, La La! French Braids!

This braid is a little more difficult than the others. For one thing, you don't start with a ponytail, so you need to hold on carefully. For another thing, it can make your arms tired if you're making really long braids!

Here's how to do a basic French braid:

1. Take a small section of hair from the top of your head. Separate it into three sections.

2. Start by crossing the sections once or twice, as though you were doing a classic braid.

3. Pick up a section of loose hair and add it to the left section. Cross that section over the center section.

4. Now pick up some loose hair and add it to the right section. Cross that section over the center.

5. Continue to repeat steps 3 and 4 until you finish the braid. Try to pull the sections tight when you add sections and when you cross them. This makes the braid look neat and last longer.

Note:

Make sure that the section of hair that you add is always the same size as or smaller than the section you're adding it to.

Something Fishy

The fish-bone braid looks harder to make than it really is. For variety, you can use a fish-bone braid instead of a classic braid in any of the hairstyles listed on the previous pages.

...ke a ponytail ...n an elastic ...d and separate ...hair into two ...n sections.

2. Take a very thin section of hair from underneath the left section. Pull it up and over the left section and add it to the right section.

3. Take a very thin section from underneath the right section. Pull it up and over the right section and add it to the left section.

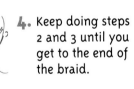

4. Keep doing steps 2 and 3 until you get to the end of the braid.

Two Important Fish-Bone Braid Tips:

1. The thinner the sections you use, the better the braid looks.
2. Pull the sections tight to keep the braid neat.

What's Up? Your Hair!

The Fun Bun

1. Make a high ponytail with an elastic band.

2. Then twist the ponytail down to the ends and wind it around the elastic.

3. Hold the hair down with bobby pins.

Stick Trick

For this style, use a chopstick or a pencil-sized hair stick.

1. Gather all your hair on the back of your head and twist it up and around several times.

If you have a hard time keeping the stick in your hair, try the same hairstyle using a butterfly clip.

2. Still holding on, fold the ends behind the twist.

3. Now weave the chopstick into and under the thickest part of the twist and keep pushing until it peeks out the other side.

Stacie collects pretty chopsticks so she can wear them in her hair.

Girls Make Curls

Curly hair is so pretty! Here's how you can set straight hair to make it curly. For all of these curling styles, make sure to start with damp hair. When your hair dries it will hold the curl.

Rock 'n' Roller

Daybreak Do

Before you go to sleep, wet your hair and make a bunch of braids all over your head. Take them out in the morning and separate them with your fingers. Your hair will be way wavy!

Midge and I used to do this at sleepover parties.

Hair rollers are a classic way to make your hair curly. The simplest rollers use Velcro to hold your hair without bobby pins. Roll a small section of damp hair around the roller from the bottom up, dabbing on a little gel. Put all your hair in rollers. Cover your head with a pretty scarf and let your curls dry. Use a blow-dryer to speed up the drying process.

Wrap Up

You can use short strips of fabric as curlers, too. Just wrap sections of wet hair around the middle of a six-inch fabric strip and tie the fabric tightly in a bow. When your hair dries, untie the bows to release your loopy new curls.

Sports Solutions

Here are some practical ideas for keeping your hair away from your face while you are exercising or playing games.

Soccer Rocker

Stacie's favorite!

Pin back your bangs and make a ponytail or pigtails. Band the pig- or ponytails with terry cloth-covered elastic bands or ribbons. For a serious sports look, add another athletic touch. Tightly roll up a cotton bandanna and tie it at the back of your head so it goes straight across your forehead.

Bandanna Mania

Here's another way bandannas can be used to keep your hair from flying around during sports: Fold a bandanna diagonally in half to make a triangle. Wrap it over your head, and tie the two corners tightly together over the third corner in the back.

Gymnastic Fantastic

Girls who flip and tumble need hair that doesn't. Gather all your hair at the top of your neck. Twist it once, flip it up, and clip at the bottom with a barrette. Bring hair upward and add a matching barrette near the top.

Snow Bunny

In wintertime a warm headwrap or earmuffs keep your ears toasty while a bouncy high ponytail keeps your hair sleek.

Christie always wears her hair like this when she's snowboarding.

Dress-up Tresses

When it's party or show time, do some grooming with your costuming!
These hairstyles work very well for costume parties and plays.

*I help my sisters when they
need ideas for costumes. Sometimes
I still dress up for Halloween!*

Fluttering Fairy

You'll need some hair gel with glitter. You can buy it, or make your
own by adding a quarter teaspoon of loose glitter to a teaspoon of
gel. Comb the glitter gel through the top layer of your hair. Then
separate your hair into two high pigtails on either side of your
head, and twist and bobby pin them into two little buns.
You can even weave strings of gold stars, tiny fabric,
or paper flowers through the buns.

Flower Girl

On flower girl duty? Leave your hair loose and create
a wreath of either silk or paper flowers. Then take
some white tulle and fasten it to half of the wreath
with bobby pins. Put the wreath on your head
and fasten it with the bobby pins.

Fairy-Tale Fancy

Make a ponytail on the very top of your head
with an elastic band. Find the thickest gold
ribbon you can. Wrap it around the ponytail
several times in a diagonal direction and
bobby pin or tie down the ribbon.
Now you're a princess!

Magical Mermaid

Brush your hair back and anchor it above your ears
with a sea-green hairband or barrettes. Now make
your locks look mermaid-wet with gel. Rub a little
gel back toward the barrettes or hairband. Brush
or curl the bottoms of your hair into the shape
of flowing ocean waves.

*Midge loves to dress
up as a mermaid.*

Storage for Hair Accessories

The Style File

When you keep your hair stuff organized, you can find what you need right away. Here are some neat ways to keep your hair accessories looking cute and organized.

Stock a Box

Stores that sell fishing equipment have metal tackle boxes that have rows of empty little plastic compartments. They're perfect for holding hair stuff. You can decorate yours by gluing charms, buttons, beads, bows, and lengths of ribbon to the outside of the box.

Skipper has one of these, and I think it's very cool.

Container Crazy

Many stores sell small see-through plastic boxes for organizing little things. Glue fabric over the boxes for decoration, or use enamel paints to write your name or paint little pictures on the outside.

Teen Totes

Look in the beauty aisle of pharmacies or large department stores for hair accessory storage ideas. There you can find brightly colored plastic carrying cases that look like large lunch boxes and are filled with compartments, trays, and drawers. You can personalize yours with paint-pens, glue, and sparkles.

You can also buy pretty fabric cosmetic bags lined with plastic. These can be used to carry or store your brushes, combs, accessories, and hair products.

Stored on a Board

Get a colored bulletin board, and ask a grown-up to hammer in several rows of nails. Then hang the board near your mirror. You can clip or drape all of your hair accessories on the nails. Tiny barrettes that don't fit can be clipped onto ribbons that you tie over the nails.

I hung one of these in Stacie's room, and she loves it!

Fun for One Is True for Two!

By now you know that caring for your hair is tons of fun, and easy—especially when you practice!

To make hair care even more interesting, try doing it with your sister, cousin, or a bud from school. Two girls can accomplish more than one on her own. Together, you'll be able to see the backs of each other's heads, help each other with braids, and tie bows onto each other's ponytails.

So invite a friend to come over for a day of hair play. Ask her to bring some cool accessories. Be creative, and never be afraid to add your own personal touch to any of the hairstyles in these pages.

I hope you now have lots of new ideas about how to make your hair even more beautiful. You should be ready to make hairstyling a part of every single day!

Keep this book handy so you can practice and maybe even try to invent some hairdos of your own! Most importantly, never forget how pretty and special you are—both inside and out!

Wanna see something fab?
Look in the mirror!

Love,
Barbie

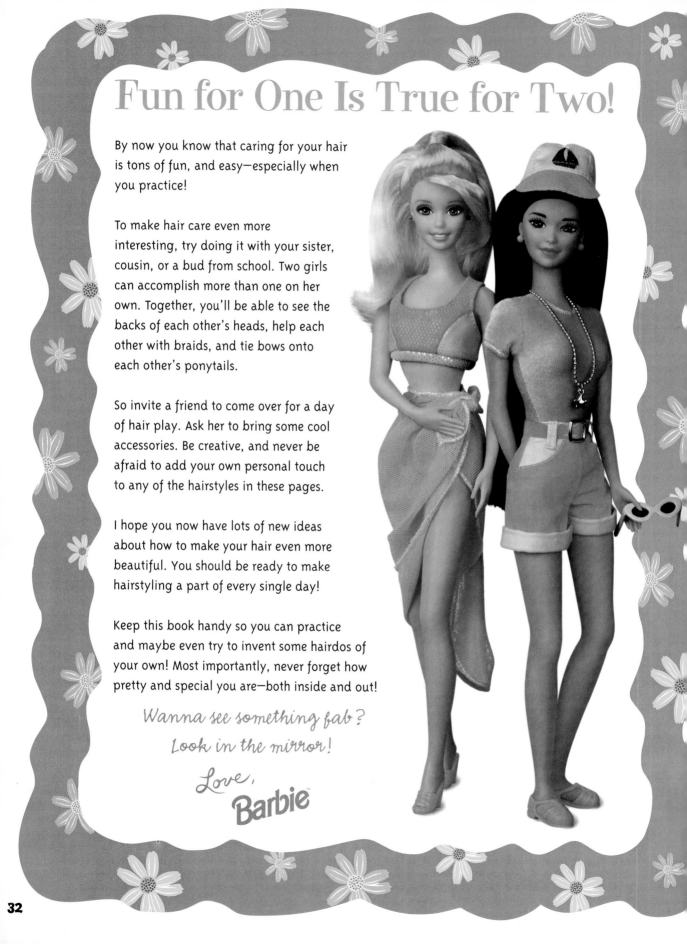